You are so loved!

♡
Jissa

PIPSQUEAK
AND THE PIGS

WRITTEN BY
LISSA WEBBER

ILLUSTRATED BY
TAMI BOYCE

FOR JONATHAN, RYAN, CLAIRE AND LADYBUG: YOU ARE THE BEST TEAMMATES EVER.

ISBN-13: 978-0-578-60012-3

ARGONNE BOOKS LLC

Johns Creek, Georgia

Though Pipsqueak always was well fed,
her siblings soared above her head!
They grew and grew and grew some more
while Pipsqueak's height stayed near the floor!

And Pipsqueak's parents disagreed
on how to best help her succeed.
"I give her food she needs to grow,"
Big Rover cried. "It's what I know."

"You have to stop," her Mama sighed.
"Without your help, she'll hit her stride."
When Rover knew that she was right,
they let Pip build an appetite.

Without Big Rover's help at lunch,
our Pip did not have much to munch!
Tall Thomas never missed his share;
his size and strength beyond compare.
Mean Horace snarled at everyone;

BRIDGET

STEVE

FRED

ED

PAULA

his bark and bite were never fun.
Then Bridget, Paula, Steve and Fred
all split their bowls and shared with Ed.
Pip stuck her nose in through the gaps,
but in the bowls were barely scraps.

Day two had Pipsqueak feeling faint!
She went for help full of complaint.
Most puppies stick to their own kind,
but Pip is of a different mind.
Her bestie is a squirrel named Chuck:
he's chunky, kind and full of pluck!

"I mean no disrespect," she said,
"but you have always been well fed.
You cannot know just how it feels
to go this long between your meals."
"It's nice to have a team," he sighed.
"Beware of having too much pride."

Well Pipsqueak did not understand
why Chuck did not lend her a hand.
She stormed away and felt so mad!
Her only friend had zilch to add.
And then she heard his voice behind,
"You're smart," he called. "Just use your mind."

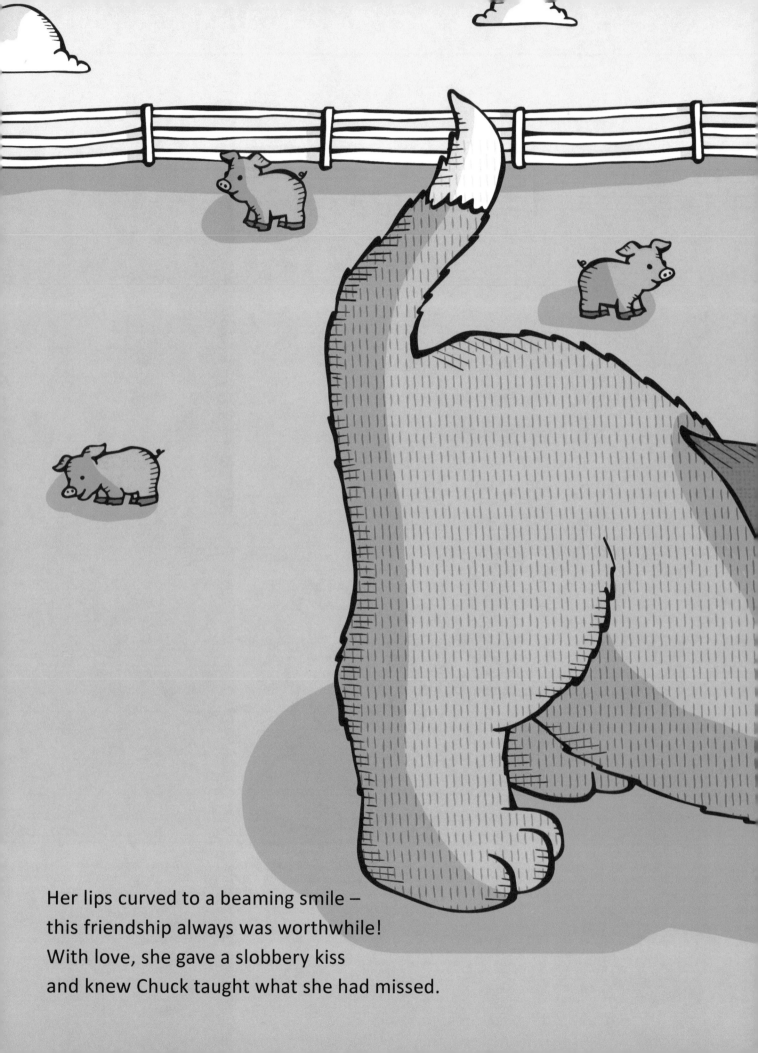

Her lips curved to a beaming smile –
this friendship always was worthwhile!
With love, she gave a slobbery kiss
and knew Chuck taught what she had missed.

While Pip is small, and not too strong,
ideas have never steered her wrong.
Chuck wiped the drool from on his face
and scratched her ear, her favorite place.

That night she got her plan correct;
her "team" was not who you'd expect!
And at the very crack of dawn
she set to work without a yawn.

The bowls for pups were near the pigs,
by food for pigs in sacks so big...

She pushed with all her might – it spilled!
The food for pigs could help her build
a sort of moat around the bowls.
This grain would help her reach her goals!

The human came to feed the dogs,
not seeing Pip between the logs.
She scrambled up to push the latch,
and pigs came out, too fast to catch!

They spread around the bowls to eat
the bulk of food right at their feet.
And Pip was small enough to fit
between the pigs, so closely knit.

She saw the bowls filled to the brim,
and scarfed her meal, her time was slim.
Just as the pigs were herded back,
she saw her siblings in a pack.

They raced up to the bowls to see
their tiny sister, full of glee!
She belched hello and wagged her tail,
no longer looking at all frail.

Her siblings were surprised, of course,
and one was mad – you guessed it, Horace!
But happy Thomas laughed out loud,
and barked "Good job!" above the crowd.

He laughed and tugged upon her tail.
"It's fun to watch you blaze your trail.
This plan of yours, it's smart, for sure.
But every day? That's not a cure.

Why not ask us to help you out?
That's what a team is all about."
Pip closed her eyes and thought of Chuck;
his thoughts had always brought her luck.

'It's nice to have a team,' he'd said,
which now she knew she had misread.
While help from strangers might be nice,
it's help from friends that happens twice.

"Let's check this out," sweet Bridget said,
and with her paw, she pulled Pip's head
right under hers, and Pip could stand!
Tall Bridget's heart was oh so grand.

From that day on they ate as one,
and always found it rather fun
to have eight paws, all side by side,
a daily friend to share a stride.

THE
END

MEET THE AUTHOR AND iLLUSTRATOR

LiSSA WEBBER is constantly inspired by her children and her writing is no exception. Their love of reading and the natural world compelled her to write stories about someone with whom they could identify: a lovable puppy whose small stature makes it hard for her to do what she wants to.

A former investment banker turned stay-at-home mama, Lissa has always loved to write. Writing happy, sweet stories with good messages for children brings her tremendous joy. All proceeds from books in the *Pipsqueak the Puppy* series are donated to Children's Healthcare of Atlanta, which holds a very special place in the family's heart. You can read more about the creation of Pipsqueak at www.pipsqueakthepuppy.com.

Lissa lives in Georgia and in addition to writing loves painting, cooking, and spending time with her family, and including sweet puppy Ladybug (pictured).

TAMi BOYCE, an illustrator and graphic designer with a fun and whimsical style, is based in Charleston, South Carolina.

"Holding a pencil in my hand has been my passion for as long as I can remember. I count myself as an extremely lucky individual because I have been able to make a career out of it. We all live in a very serious world, and I like to use my quirky style to remind us of the love, joy, and humor that is often overlooked around us."

To see more of Tami's work, visit tamiboyce.com.

CPSIA information can be obtained
at www.ICGtesting.com
Printed in the USA
BVHW062237261119
564888BV00002B/18/P